Ages 3-7

COME ONE!
COME ALL!

Be our **guest**
at the **fest**
where the **test**
is to find which **pest**
is the **best** –
or at **least**
a better **pest**

THAN ALL THE
REST!

Julia Durango never fully appreciated bugs until her oldest son went through a phase where his nightly bedtime story was a guide to insects and spiders. She now has the utmost respect for bugs and avoids squishing them whenever possible. Julia is the author of DREAM HOP, illustrated by Jared Lee; CHA-CHA CHIMPS, illustrated by Eleanor Taylor; and most recently, ANGELS WATCHING OVER ME, illustrated by Elisa Kleven. She lives with her favorite pests, sons Kyle and Ryan, in Ottawa, Illinois.

Kurt Cyrus has a very different relationship with the pests in his life. He and his pooch, Osa, have perfected what Kurt likes to call the "whack and gulp" technique. (Osa does the gulping. So flies, consider yourselves WARNED!) When not showing pesky pests who's boss, Kurt does an awesome job of drawing them and just about any other kind of critter you can think of. From the bugs of ODDHOPPER OPERA and the marine life of HOTEL DEEP (two picture books that Kurt also wrote), to the mammoths of MAMMOTHS ON THE MOVE and the cows in SIXTEEN COWS (both written by Lisa Wheeler), to the rock-and-roll legend Buddy Holly in Anne Bustard's BUDDY, there isn't a varmint born that Kurt can't draw! Kurt lives in Cottage Grove, Oregon, with his wife, Linnea.

Jacket design by Einav Aviram
Jacket illustrations copyright © 2007 by Kurt Cyrus
Manufactured in the United States of America

Visit us on the World Wide Web
www.SimonSaysKids.com

Simon & Schuster
Books for Young Readers
Simon & Schuster, New York

For Barry Goldblatt and Kevin Lewis,
the bee's knees of the children's
book world—J. D.

Pest Fest

By **JULIA DURANGO**

Illustrated by **KURT CYRUS**

Simon & Schuster Books for Young Readers
New York London Toronto Sydney

"Pest Fest! Pest Fest!"

the Carpet Beetle barked.

"The talent show is set to go.

The bets are placed; come on, make haste!

Let's start the annual Pest Fest!"

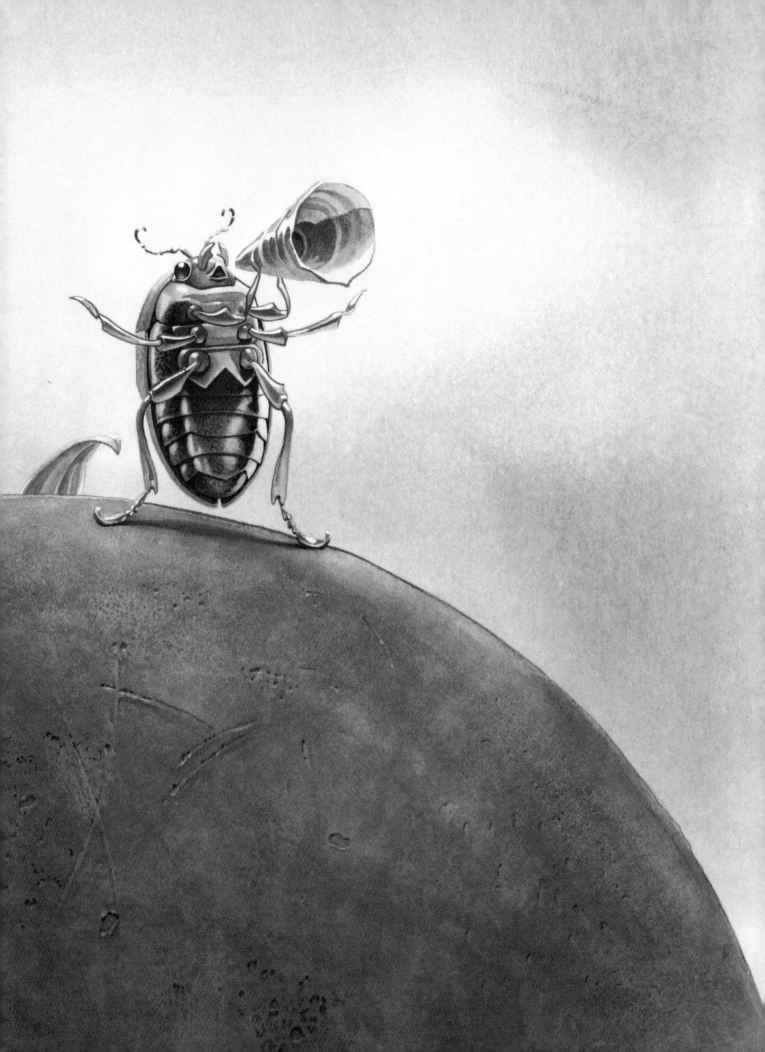

The first one up was Ladybug,
who sang a charming tune:
"I'm such a lovely, dainty bug,
I make the Manbugs swoon."

"Oh, piffle!" sniffled Butterfly,
who hovered overhead.
"In beauty pageants far and wide,
I'm sure to win instead."

"Why, that's abz-zurd!" buzzed Honeybee,
who whizzed down from the sky.
"There's none so stunning as my queen,
and Honeybees don't lie."

"Dear me!" the little Housefly moaned.
"I cannot hope to win.
My looks would rate a zero
on a scale from one to ten."

"Pest Fest! Pest Fest!"

the Carpet Beetle barked.

"Good looks are great, but get it straight,

they matter not a diddly-squat!

This is a **TALENT** contest!"

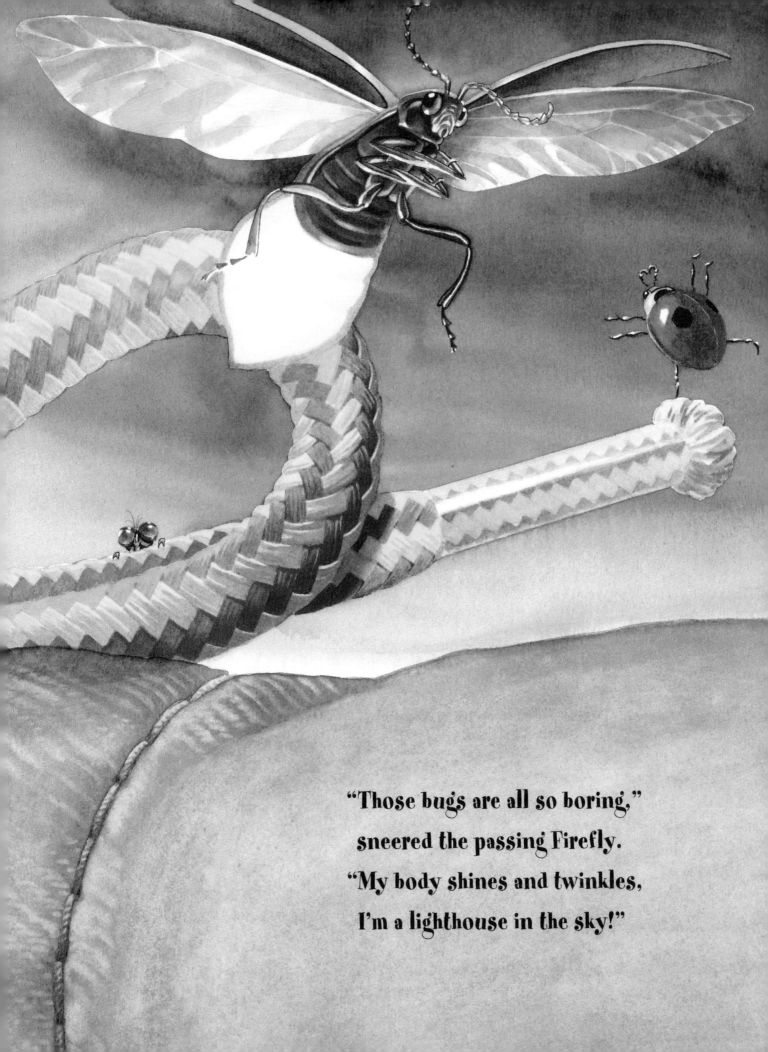

"Those bugs are all so boring,"
sneered the passing Firefly.
"My body shines and twinkles,
I'm a lighthouse in the sky!"

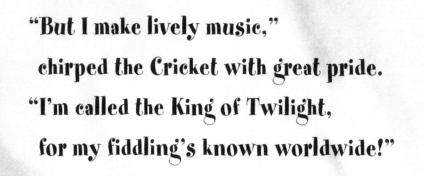

"But I make lively music,"
chirped the Cricket with great pride.
"I'm called the King of Twilight,
for my fiddling's known worldwide!"

"Malarkey!" the Cicada called.
"My shrilling fame is greater.
My racket is much louder,
I'm an expert noise creator!"

"Oh my!" The little Housefly sighed.
"It's time for me to quit.
I can't compete with these fine bugs—
I'm dreadfully unfit."

"Pest Fest! Pest Fest!"
the Carpet Beetle barked.
"They brag, they shout, they rant, they pout.
(Give us a break, our eardrums ache!)
They want to pass the Pest Test!"

"Phoo-hooey!" huffed the Spider
from her sticky web estate.
"My thread's the best across the land,
and count my legs—I've eight!"

"It's quality," snapped Grasshopper,
"not quantity that rules.
My legs can bounce me to the moon
and back again, you fools!"

"Ahoy there," hailed the Water Strider,
showing off his stroke.
"Prepare to sink, landlubbing grubs.
You humbugs are a joke!"

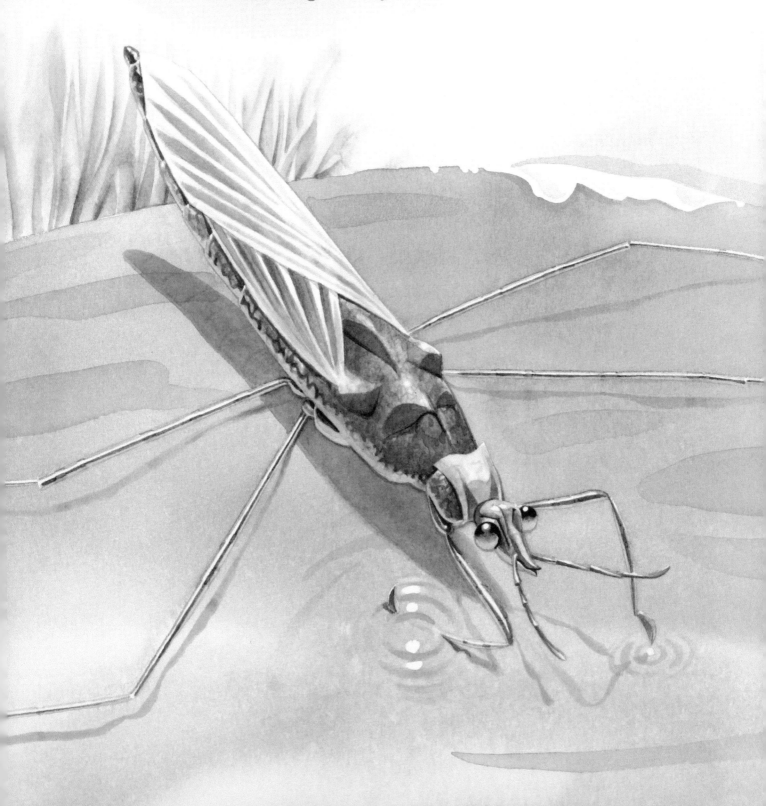

"My word!" the little Housefly wailed.
"I've lost the game for sure.
I'm nowhere near as skillful–
I'm a hopeless amateur!"

"Pest Fest! Pest Fest!"

the Carpet Beetle barked.

"There's one last chance for smarty-pants

to play the game, before we name

the bug who'll be the Best Pest!"

"No thanks," the little Housefly said.
"I'm sure it would be fun.
But when it comes to talent,
I'm afraid that I have none."

"No talent?" gasped the insects.
"How unfortunate! How bleak!
Why, surely there is something
you can do that is unique!"

The Housefly sniffled sadly,
and he shook his hairy head.
"The only thing I do all day
is hang around," he said.

"I pester dogs, I bother cats
(I find them rather lazy).
I make the bulls see red,
and drive them absolutely crazy."

"Pest Fest! Pest Fest!"

the Carpet Beetle barked.

"Young matador, please tell us more—
but make it quick. We need to pick
the winner of the Pest Fest!"

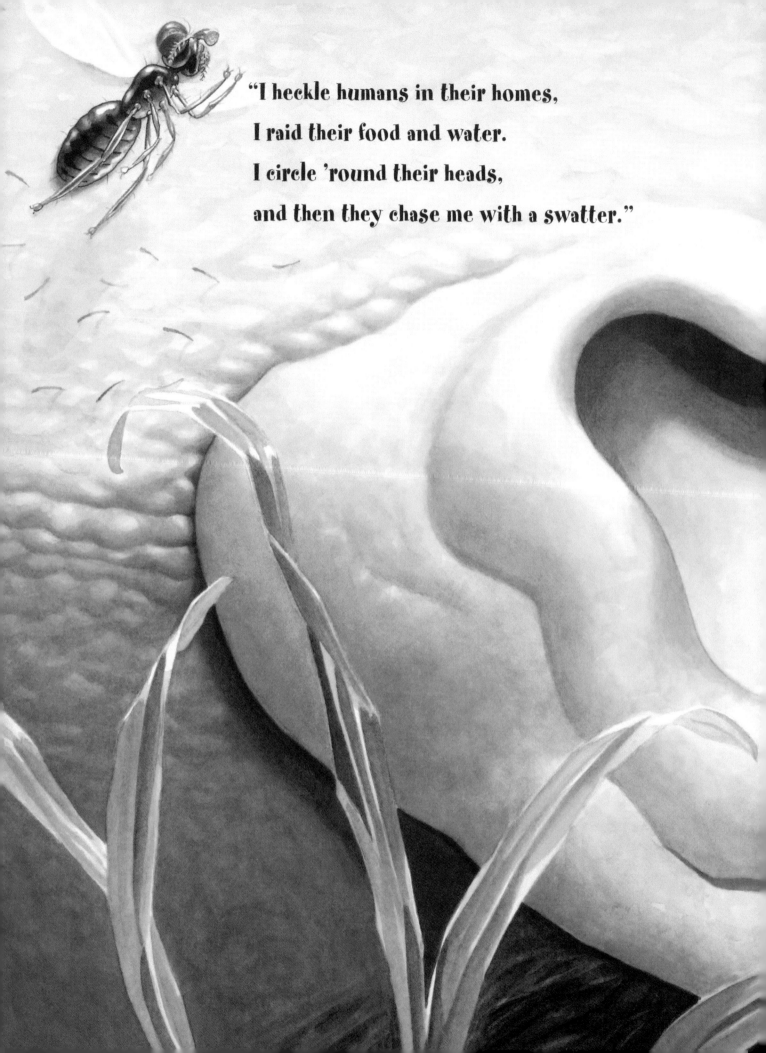

"I heckle humans in their homes,
I raid their food and water.
I circle 'round their heads,
and then they chase me with a swatter."

The Housefly wept in shame
until the Carpet Beetle said,
"But surely you must see, dear Fly,
the gifts you have instead . . .

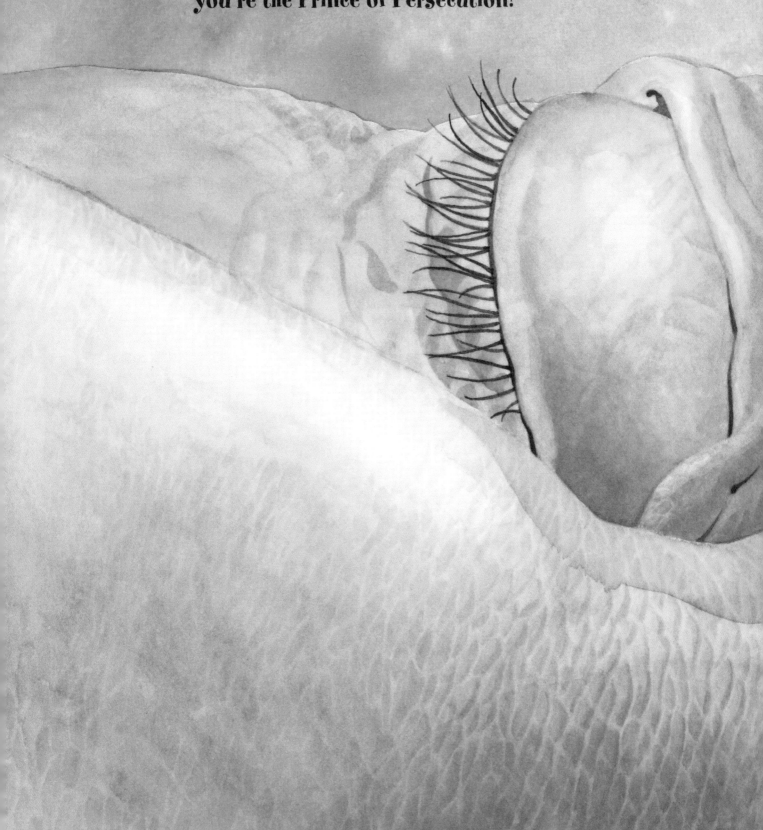

. . . a knack for being pesky,
you're a breeder of pollution,
you're the ace of aggravation,
you're the Prince of Persecution!"

The humble Housefly grinned,
and then the bugs let out a cheer:
"Hip-hip-hooray, the Housefly wins!

"The Best Pest of the Year!"

SIMON & SCHUSTER BOOKS FOR YOUNG READERS
An imprint of Simon & Schuster Children's Publishing Division
1230 Avenue of the Americas, New York, New York 10020
Text copyright © 2007 by Julia Durango
Illustrations copyright © 2007 by Kurt Cyrus
All rights reserved, including the right of reproduction in whole or in part in any form.
SIMON & SCHUSTER BOOKS FOR YOUNG READERS is a trademark of Simon & Schuster, Inc.
Book design by Einav Aviram
The text for this book is set in Spumoni.
The illustrations for this book are rendered in watercolor and colored pencils.
Manufactured in the United States of America
2 4 6 8 10 9 7 5 3
CIP data for this book is available from the Library of Congress.
ISBN-13: 978-1-4424-3095-2

CPSIA information can be obtained
at www.ICGtesting.com
Printed in the USA
LVIC05n1622091214
418019LV00007B/47